KIDS CAN'T STOP READING
THE CHOOSE YOUR
OWN ADVENTURE® STORIES!

"Choose Your Own Adventure is the best thing that has come along since books themselves."
—Alysha Beyer, age 11

"I didn't read much before, but now I read my Choose Your Own Adventure books almost every night."
—Chris Brogan, age 13

"I love the control I have over what happens next."
—Kosta Efstathiou, age 17

"Choose Your Own Adventure books are so much fun to read and collect—I want them all!"
—Brendan Davin, age 11

And teachers like this series, too:
"We have read and reread, worn thin, loved, loaned, bought for others, and donated to school libraries our Choose Your Own Adventure books."

CHOOSE YOUR OWN ADVENTURE®—
AND MAKE READING MORE FUN!

Bantam Books in the Choose Your Own Adventure® series
Ask your bookseller for the books you have missed

HIJACKED!

BY RICHARD BRIGHTFIELD

ILLUSTRATED BY FRANK BOLLE

An Edward Packard Book

BANTAM BOOKS
NEW YORK • TORONTO • LONDON • SYDNEY • AUCKLAND

RL 4, age 10 and up

HIJACKED!
A Bantam Book / October 1990

CHOOSE YOUR OWN ADVENTURE® is a registered trademark of Bantam Books, a division of Bantam Doubleday Dell Publishing Group, Inc. Registered in U.S. Patent and Trademark Office and elsewhere.

Original conception of Edward Packard

Cover art by Romas Kukalis
Interior illustrations by Frank Bolle

ISBN 0-553-28635-8

Published simultaneously in the United States and Canada

PRINTED IN THE UNITED STATES OF AMERICA

OPM   0 9 8 7 6 5 4 3 2

**For Susan Korman
and Charles Kochman**

WARNING!!!

Do not read this book straight through from beginning to end. These pages contain many different adventures that you may have when your school bus is hijacked! From time to time as you read along, you will be asked to make a choice. Your choice may lead to success or disaster!

The adventures you have are the results of your choices. You are responsible because you choose! After you make a choice, follow the instructions to see what happens to you next.

Think carefully before you make a decision. Once you are hijacked, your life is in great danger. Even if you do manage to escape from the hijackers and alert the authorities, it doesn't necessarily mean that you'll be safe!

Good luck!

It's finally Friday afternoon, and you're sitting in school with one more class to go. You've packed your books, and you're staring at your watch as the minutes tick away. Your social studies teacher, Mrs. Myers, is going on and on with her lecture about international terrorism. You couldn't be less interested. When the bell finally rings, you're up from your seat and out the door before it stops.

Outside, you meet your friends Sally and Dan, and the three of you leave together, heading for the school bus.

"Let's sit in the back, away from Buzzy Hargrove," Sally says. "He always gives Mrs. Wilson a hard time while she's driving."

"If Buzzy makes any more trouble for her, he's going to be barred from the bus permanently," Dan says, "and his parents will have to pick him up from school every day."

You, Sally, and Dan get on the bus and go to the back. You get the window seat. Minutes later, Mrs. Wilson is already calling for order. "Everybody calm down!" she shouts as she starts the motor and closes the door. Slowly she pulls out of the school parking lot, pauses for a moment at the stop sign on Main Street, and then carefully turns into traffic.

Turn to page 2.

"Buzzy, stay in your seat," Mrs. Wilson says.

"I just wanted to get some class notes from Tom. I'm doing my homework on the bus," Buzzy says, grinning.

"One more disturbance, Buzzy Hargrove, and you're going to be *walking* home."

Six blocks later the bus stops to let off a few students. Anyone who lives closer than six blocks is officially a "walker" and can't use the bus.

The bus continues on, turns right onto Chestnut Street, makes a few more stops, and then starts down the long stretch toward Fair Street.

Suddenly Mrs. Wilson slams on the brakes, almost throwing you out of your seat. You manage to protect yourself by grabbing on to the seat in front of you, but your schoolbooks and papers go flying. You look down the aisle and through the front window. A truck is in front of the bus, blocking the road. Mrs. Wilson's quick thinking and fast reflexes were able to keep the bus from crashing into it.

She opens the front door of the bus and starts hollering at the truck driver. For a few moments the kids on the bus are stunned into silence—then they start screaming and hollering. All is pandemonium. You look out the back. You can hardly believe what you are seeing.

Several armed men wearing khaki fatigues and ski masks are running toward the bus. You turn and see two more come out of the truck ahead. One of them jumps on the bus and points a gun at Mrs. Wilson.

Go on to the next page.

"What's going on?" Sally asks.

"I don't know," you say. "Maybe they're filming a movie. It sure looks like one."

"Everyone back in their seats," the man in the mask orders, only he gets about as much response as Mrs. Wilson does when she says the same thing. He fires a machine-gun burst into the roof of the bus. The sound is deafening. All of your classmates are in their seats in seconds. "All right, drive," the masked man says to Mrs. Wilson. "Turn left at the next corner."

"You won't get away with this, whoever you are," she says, giving the man the same distasteful look she usually gives to the students.

"Shut up and drive," the man says.

Mrs. Wilson puts the bus in gear and takes it to the next corner.

"Faster!" the man orders, stamping down on Mrs. Wilson's foot on the accelerator. The bus turns the corner and lurches down a side street, narrowly missing two parked cars. Halfway down the block, the man orders Mrs. Wilson out of her seat and takes over the driving. He makes a sudden right turn down a little-used street leading to the old, abandoned railroad station. Looking ahead, you can see a huge van, the kind used to carry big loads of furniture. The bus is heading for the back of the van at full speed. You scrunch down in your seat, preparing for the crash.

Turn to page 9.

4

"Okay, let's hide," you say. Dan decides not to risk it. As quickly as you can you grab Sally's hand and pull her underneath the bus. The two of you crouch behind one of the large front tires as the two gunmen drag poor Buzzy, still screaming and hollering, off the bus and outside.

A moment later, one of the hijackers comes back and goes inside the bus. You can hear his footsteps over your head. You realize that he is checking the spaces under the seats. You hold your breath, wondering if he will check under the bus too.

He gets off the bus and quickly shines his flashlight around underneath. Luckily he's in a big hurry and misses the two of you. He then takes off, running down the ramp and off the van. Seconds later, the ramp is raised and slammed shut. You feel the movement as the van starts off again.

You and Sally crawl out from under the bus. The inside of the van is dark, but there is one thin crack of light at the side of the rear door. You put your eye to it and look out. You can't see much, but as the van pulls away, you can see that the gunmen have lined up your classmates outside. As the van turns slightly, you catch a momentary glimpse of Dan and the others being loaded into a truck.

"Let's get back in the bus and sit down," you say as your eyes gradually get used to the dim light.

Turn to page 67.

6

"Okay," you say to Dr. Cranshaw, trusting him. "I'll join."

The nurse helps Dr. Cranshaw untie you. Then she brings you a wheelchair. They push you out of the infirmary, down a long corridor, and into a large amphitheater filled with members of the International Fighters for Freedom. At the front, standing on a platform, is Carlos, their leader. He raises his arm in a fascist salute, and the crowd shouts their support.

Carlos soon sees you. Slowly he comes down from the platform and walks up the center aisle until he stands in front of you. He takes a metal scepter from under his jacket and places it on your head.

You feel an electric shock go through your body. At the same time, you see a blinding flash of light that seems to come from inside your head, behind your eyes.

"Welcome to the International Fighters for Freedom. You are now one of us," Carlos announces, and walks back to the platform.

You sit there, unable to move. Every time you try to think about what is happening, you see another flash of light.

"Don't worry," Dr. Cranshaw whispers, "you'll soon learn *not* to think."

The End

Looking carefully through the narrow space between two backseats, you see several men outside behind the van. They're no longer wearing their ski masks.

"We better get rid of this bus as soon as we can," you hear one of the men say. "Dump it into one of the deep pits."

"I'll get a work crew together right away," another one says. The men leave, heading down a side corridor.

"Deep pits! We'd better get off of this bus— fast!" you say.

Cautiously you and Sally climb off the bus and run down the ramp behind the van. You realize you are in a dimly lit natural cavern of some sort. Stalactites, long fingers of stone, hang down from the high ceiling. Except in a few places, there are no stalagmites pointing up from the floor. Instead it's paved over with cement.

Turn to page 14.

Suddenly the rear door of the van drops down and forms a ramp. The driver brakes a bit and, with a bump, drives the bus up into the van. The back door of the van swings closed, plunging all of you into total darkness.

The masked driver gets up and snaps on a flashlight. He opens the door of the bus and lets in another man. For the first time ever on the bus everyone sits in silence, stunned by what has happened.

The hijacker shoves Mrs. Wilson back in the driver's seat, although it's obvious she isn't going to be driving anywhere with the bus now inside the van. "I won't put up with this, I simply won't," she says before the hijackers put a gag over her mouth and tie her hands to the steering wheel.

You can feel your heart pounding. What are they going to do to us? you wonder as a chill goes up your back. You feel the van start moving—slowly at first, making several turns, then speeding up.

After what seems like hours, the van makes a sharp turn off the highway and starts down a bumpy road. Finally it comes to a stop. The back opens, and the inside of the bus is bathed in light.

Turn to page 113.

The police station is a one-story brick building. You and Sally walk in the front door and over to the front desk. "Hello?" you call out, but there's no response. You start back out the door. As you do, a patrol car skids to a stop in front. A single policeman jumps out and runs over to you.

"You must be the two strangers who were reported wandering around town," he says matter-of-factly.

"We weren't *wandering*," Sally says. "We came to town to report a crime."

"And what might that be?" the policeman asks.

"Our school bus was hijacked, and we were kidnapped," you say.

"You look all right to me," the policeman says.

"Of course we do," Sally says. "We escaped."

"And where might these alleged hijackers be now?" he asks.

"They have a headquarters in a cavern up in the mountains not far from here," you say.

"I see," the policeman says. "Well, I'm a bit shorthanded right now. I'll have to get some help. In the meantime, I'm going to have to lock you up in my holding cell in the back."

"Lock *us* up!" Sally exclaims.

Go on to the next page.

"It's for your own protection," the policeman says. "You don't want the hijackers to come back and kidnap you again before I get back, do you?"

"I don't want to be locked up," you say. "Listen, we'll take care of ourselves."

"Let me put it this way," the policeman says, drawing his gun. "I'm holding the two of you as material witnesses whether you like it or not." With that he forces you and Sally at gunpoint into the cell and slams the door shut.

Turn to page 55.

Seconds later, you are through the door and inside a small, unlit room. Against the wall on one side is a ladder leading up to a trapdoor in the ceiling. You point to it and pantomime going up. Sally nods.

You are about to start up when you hear a commotion coming from the cavern. Orders are being shouted back and forth as the school bus is backed out of the van and over to a wide opening in the opposite wall. Several men are standing next to it. Two of them are dressed in policemen's uniforms.

"Look at that," you whisper. "Some of the police must be involved in this."

The men, including the two in uniform, take hold of the outside of the bus and manage to push it through the opening. You hear it tumbling end over end bouncing off the walls as it falls. That must be one of the deep pits they were talking about, you reason. The sounds fade out somewhere far below.

Backing away from the door of the small room, you start up the ladder, shaking slightly. You push up on the trapdoor, but nothing happens. You push again, this time with all your might, but you can't budge it. Then you feel around the edge and find a small latch.

Turn to page 68.

As you eat, you tell Thur all about the hijacking and how you managed to escape from the caverns.

"I suspected something like this would happen with those people. They've gone way over the line this time. Come, after you've finished eating, I'll show you something interesting," Thur says, chuckling.

You quickly down the last of your oatmeal, asking for seconds, you're so hungry. When you're finished, Thur leads you to the back of the little house and pulls open a trapdoor in the floor. "This is my secret entrance to the caverns. Branches of the caverns reach the surface in different places. One day I discovered that my house was built right over one. No one knows about it. Come, I'll show you."

Do you really want to go with Thur back to the caverns? you wonder. It's been all you could do to get away from there. Perhaps you should continue on, away from them and Thur.

If you decide to go back to the caverns, turn to page 66.

If you decide to leave Thur and go on your way, turn to page 74.

You look around for a place to hide. You're in luck. Not far from the van is a cavelike indentation in the wall partially hidden by a few remaining stalagmites. You and Sally rush over, looking up and down the cavern at the same time. In one direction you see people moving around at the far end. In the other, a guard is leaning back in his chair, propped against the rough wall. He looks like he's asleep, but it's difficult to tell for sure.

At the far end of the cavern you can hear the sound of voices getting closer. You and Sally carefully peek between two stalagmites. A group of heavily armed men is coming in your direction. You duck down as the procession makes a right turn in front of you and heads down a side corridor.

"We have to get out of here," Sally says. "Do you think we could sneak past the guard? The outside door could be in that direction."

"We may be able to get past him, but it might be too well guarded on the other side," you say. "If we go down the other way, one of those side corridors might lead to a way out."

Either decision, you realize, is risky.

If you try to sneak past the guard,
turn to page 60.

If you go deeper into the cavern,
turn to page 37.

The landscape is breathtaking. Far across the woods and farms you can see blue, hazy mountains on the distant horizon. The hijackers might have lookouts posted outside, you realize, so you duck down behind some nearby bushes. From there, you look around carefully.

You are at the top of a high hill. Off in the distance you can see a small town where a few tall buildings and several church steeples rise up out of the trees. Your guess is that it's Gloveville, the town you went through on the way to the caverns. You can see a dirt road that leads from the direction of the town to a spot partway down the hill, vanishing into the hillside—the entrance to the cavern. In the distance you can see a highway.

Down and off to the right is the edge of a thick woods. Turning the other way, you can see several farms with herds of cows, neat white farmhouses, and large red barns.

"If we go to the town, we can get the police," Sally says. "The news of the hijacking must be on the radio by now."

"I don't know," you say. "Remember the two policemen we saw in the caverns? They could be from the town. I think we have to be really careful. If we go over to the woods, we might be able to find a way out of here and avoid the town altogether."

If you decide to go toward the town,
turn to page 56.

If you decide to go toward the woods,
turn to page 105.

The palm trees along the shore give way to cypress, all thickly covered with vines and moss. The ground is spongy and flooded in some places.

"Do you think the beach patrol comes down this far?" Dan asks.

"I don't know. We'll just have to lie low and be careful," you say.

You curl up among the vines, so thickly intertwined that they make a natural hammock. Soon the two of you drift off to sleep.

Later, bright sunlight wakes you. You carefully look out through the bushes toward the beach. There's a cabin cruiser anchored just offshore. You can clearly see a man on deck examining the shore with binoculars. You quickly duck down, though you're pretty sure he can't see you through the thick vegetation.

"What is it?" Dan asks, waking up.

"A boat—offshore. It could be the hijackers hunting for us."

"What should we do?"

"Well, we can hide right here and hope that Jimmy made it to the mainland," you suggest. "Or we can go deeper into the jungle and try to find some kind of wild fruit to live on." Whatever your decision, you realize it may be your last.

If you stay where you are, turn to page 109.

If you go deeper into the jungle, turn to page 31.

You and Sally jump in. Seconds later, the back door of the truck slams shut, and you hear a click. "Hey, you don't have to lock it!" you call out, banging on the inside of the door. You hear the driver laugh as he starts the truck up, makes a U-turn, and heads back toward Gloveville.

Soon the truck is back at the caverns. The door is opened, and the hijackers drag you out, taking Sally off in one direction and you in the other.

You are thrown into a bare, windowless cell that is carved in the rock. For the next four days, you are fed only tasteless gruel pushed through a small opening at the base of the door.

Eventually the cell door is opened. You stagger to your feet. Sally is standing there, dressed in a khaki uniform like the ones the terrorists are wearing. She seems to be drugged.

"What have they done to you!" you exclaim.

"I came to say good-bye," she says. "I have joined the IFF to fight for world freedom. I told Carlos, our leader, that you could never be converted to our great cause. Therefore, you must be terminated."

"Terminated!" you scream. "Sally, you can't let them do that to me!"

You rush toward Sally, but the door is slammed in your face. A short time later, they come for you.

The End

"Get down, quick!" you whisper.

The two of you dive behind some nearby rocks. The light sweeps across the area where you were just standing. In the distance, in the direction of the cavern door, you hear the crackle of walkie-talkies again. The light then sweeps in the other direction and blinks out.

You are about to get up when you hear distant shouts. Several cars come out of the underground hideout, their headlights cutting into the darkness.

"They've spotted us!" Sally says in a panic.

"No, I don't think so. Someone else must have tried to escape," you say calmly.

"If they did, I hope they try to escape in the opposite direction."

You and Sally stay where you are until all is quiet again. It is now nighttime, but the rising moon gives enough light for you to make your way over to the woods. You stand at the edge for a second, taking a deep breath, then the two of you go in among the trees.

Turn to page 84.

Several guards patrol the aisle of the plane, keeping everyone in check. You wait awhile, then carefully slip your hand up to the edge of the window. You push the curtain back just a bit, exposing a tiny corner. Then you let your head slump to the wall and pretend to be asleep.

You keep your right eye closed and look out the window with the other. You are flying over the ocean! A short time later you sneak another look. You are still over the water, but you are coming upon an island. The plane is already banking to the left and beginning its descent.

After it lands, everyone is ushered off in single file and made to line up in the bright sunlight. The air is hot and humid. You see palm trees all around. You must be somewhere in the tropics.

A crowd of unarmed figures in army-style fatigues waits just outside the plane. They divide the lot of you up into groups. Several of the figures—some are men and some are women—herd the group you and Dan are in off to one side of the airfield.

"Each group will be assigned an instructor," one of the guards says. "It will be explained to you in time why you were brought here."

Turn to page 91.

You decide to take the chance. You and Sally go out into the clearing across from the man. He jumps as you come out of the shadows and into the firelight, revealing yourselves.

"Don't be afraid," Sally calls out. "We're just lost."

"You startled me," the man says. "My name is Jason." He continues to roast marshmallows. "Would you like some?"

You both nod. "How'd you get lost?" he asks, handing you each a marshmallow.

"Our school bus was hijacked, but we managed to escape," you explain, telling him the whole story.

"My, my. It sounds complicated," Jason says. "Well, why don't you spend the night with me and in the morning we'll go to the police. I went through a town called Gloveville on the way here and—"

"We're not sure about the police in Gloveville," Sally says. "We think some of them might be in with the hijackers."

"We'd rather go to the police in another town— farther away," you say.

You can see from the look on Jason's face that he doesn't quite believe you.

"News of the hijacking is probably on the radio and television by now," Sally says. "You can check if you don't believe us."

Go on to the next page.

"I've been out here fishing and camping all day—trying to get away from bad news," Jason says. "I didn't bring a radio."

"We really need your help," Sally says.

"I can see that," Jason says. "But there's not much any of us can do tonight. I was just about to turn in. My tent is set up over there. I have some extra blankets in the car. If you like, you can use them."

"Thanks, that'll be great," Sally says. "I hate to ask this since you're being so kind to us, but do you have anything to eat besides marshmallows?"

"I have some cheese sandwiches back in the car. I'll go get them," Jason says. A few minutes later he's back, and only a minute later you're both finished eating, ready to turn in for the night.

As the fire dies down, you and Sally curl up in the blankets next to Jason's tent.

Turn to page 80.

"This your family?" the officer asks Jason, pointing to you and Sally.

"Sure is," Jason says.

"Did you see any hitchhikers?" the man asks. "There's a couple of kids—escaped from the state reformatory. Dangerous characters. They look innocent enough, but they're wanted for murder."

"Murder?" Jason gasps.

"Hard to believe, isn't it?" the officer says with a sigh. "Kids these days."

Jason continues to drive, relieved to be let go. When he gets to Gloveville he stops in front of a convenience store. You quickly run in and buy the morning paper and some sodas.

Back in the car, all of you look at the newspaper. The whole front page is taken up with news about the hijacking.

"You were right," Jason says. "To tell you the truth, I had some doubts about what you'd told me."

You turn to the story inside. There are pictures of some of the hijacked kids. You and Sally are included. "Oh great," you say. "The hijackers are going to see this and realize that we've escaped. We'd better get out of this town fast."

Turn to page 32.

After the meal, Lania leads you and your group out of the dining tent and over to a series of one-story buildings not far from the beach. Inside are large rooms with bunks.

"You can rest here or go down to the beach, if you'd like, but you are *not* to cross the rope fence at each end. I will start your reeducation program tomorrow," Lania says as she goes off.

"I wonder what she means by *reeducation,*" Dan asks.

"I think it's what our social studies teacher, Mrs. Myers, calls brainwashing," you say. "They decide what they want you to believe and then they *make* you believe it, without you realizing what they are doing."

"They'll never make me believe in something I don't want to," Dan says.

"I wouldn't be too sure," you say. "According to Mrs. Myers, they have their methods."

"Oh, great," Dan says. "We've got to get out of here."

Turn to page 81.

One of the officers gets out and comes over. "A little over the speed limit, weren't you?" he says, taking out his book. "My radar clocked you in at ninety miles an hour."

You and Sally get out of the car. "We're escaping from some hijackers," you say. "Really, officer, we are! You've probably seen it in the paper. Look, we have a copy right here."

"I've heard some fancy excuses for speeding but—" the officer starts. At that moment, the patrol car from Gloveville pulls up, and two men dressed in police uniforms jump out.

"We'll take over, officers," one of them says. "These two kids are criminals. We have to take them back to Gloveville."

"They're lying," you say, realizing that your suspicions were right. "They're in with the hijackers."

"There *was* a school bus hijacked," the Denver policeman says. "We've been told to be on the lookout for it."

"Listen, we can't waste time arguing. We have to get them back," the Gloveville policeman says, going for his gun.

"Don't even think about it," says the other city officer standing next to his patrol car with a shotgun in his hand.

"You're going to be in big trouble," the Gloveville policeman says.

"We'll see who's going to be in trouble," the city officer says. "Once you cross the Denver city line you are in our jurisdiction."

Turn to page 88.

In a clearing ahead stands a small, almost minia-ture, house. It has a sharply peaked roof and is decorated all over with brightly painted wooden scrollwork. A faint wisp of smoke comes out of its stone chimney.

You walk over and stare for a few minutes, al-most speechless. Then you call out, "Is anyone home?"

The top half of the small Dutch door in front pops open, and a white-bearded head looks out. "Yes? Can I help you?" the man asks.

"Well . . . we're . . . sort of . . ." you start.

"Lost in the woods? Is that it? You kids are al-ways getting lost in the woods." The man opens the rest of the door and walks all the way outside. You can hardly believe it—he is about three feet tall.

"Well, we're not exactly lost," Sally says, look-ing at him in amazement. "We just escaped from some hijackers over in the caverns and—"

"You mean from those miserable underground varmints?" he says. "Well, in that case, come in-side."

Turn to page 36.

"That can't be," you say. "We saw—"

"Hey Sarge," one of the policemen says, running into the room. "These kids are right. A search crew just found the remains of the school bus at the bottom of a two-hundred-foot pit inside the caverns."

The FBI men take you and Sally into another room.

"We're sorry we had to put you through the rough questioning," one of them says. "But you see, we had to be sure you weren't in with the terrorists."

"Terrorists?" you say. "Those hijackers were terrorists?"

"Yes. They're a group that calls themselves IFF, International Fighters for Freedom," the agent says.

"They sure fight for freedom in a strange kind of way," Sally says.

"You're right," the FBI man says. "Unfortunately, your lives are still in danger. For the time being, we're sending you to an isolated farmhouse in the country where you'll be safe. The house is heavily guarded. Two of our best men will go with you. Your parents and friends can talk to you on the security phone whenever you want."

Turn to page 61.

"Let's get as far away from the beach as we can," you say.

There are no real paths through the swampy jungle, but you make your way on pieces of springy land and along the trunks of fallen trees. After a while, you stop to rest. "This looks like it might be edible," Dan says, plucking a plum-shaped fruit from a nearby vine.

"It could also be poisonous," you say.

"Not if it tastes good. I'll take a tiny bite," Dan says. "Not bad. Strange—but good. Here, try one."

Turn to page 51.

Jason gets back on the main highway, heading for the next town. Suddenly you hear a siren. It's a patrol car coming up fast behind you. It pulls beside Jason. The officer inside motions for him to pull over.

"What now?" Jason says rhetorically. "I wasn't speeding."

"I think we're in trouble," Sally says.

"These may or may not be real police," you whisper to Jason. "They could be some of the hijackers in police uniforms. They may have recognized us from the papers."

"I could try and outrun them," Jason whispers.

You realize that Jason's car is probably powerful enough to make a getaway. On the other hand, you might get caught and wind up in serious trouble.

If you ask Jason to make a run for it, turn to page 63.

If you decide it's too dangerous, turn to page 38.

You and Sally follow Bob up the beach to where George is collecting driftwood.

"I don't know where all this comes from, but fortunately it washes up on the beach," George says. "I get a fire going by rubbing two sticks together."

"That really works?" Sally asks.

"Nothing to it," George says. "Watch this." He stoops down and puts the pointed end of a thin, round piece of wood into a depression in another piece of wood on the ground. Then he rubs his hands together with the thin piece between them, creating a kind of drill. He does this furiously for a while until you see a tiny spark glow in the wood dust ground out in the depression. Then, without stopping, he carefully blows on the spark until the wood dust catches fire. He transfers the flame to a pile of wood shavings, gradually adding small sticks.

"That's fantastic!" Sally exclaims.

Turn to page 46.

You see Lania dimly in the darkness and run after her as she goes rapidly up the beach. She stops next to a grove of palm trees. "Over here," she whispers, disappearing into the grove. You follow her. There, resting upside down, is a large rowboat.

"We must get this turned over and drag it down to the water," she says. "Come on, we haven't that much time."

The boat is heavy. It's all the three of you can do to turn it over and drag it along the sand to the surf. No wonder Lania needed your help.

"This is the hardest part," she says. "We have to get the boat through the surf and out into the ocean. It has to be timed just right. Now when I say go, push the boat straight out."

A wave breaks on the shore, washing in up to your knees. "Go!" Lania says.

The three of you push for all you're worth. The boat glides forward as another wave starts to build up just offshore. The boat gets to it just as it crests. For a moment, the boat—with the three of you clinging on to it—hangs on the top of the wave; then it slides down the other side.

"That was close!" Lania calls over. "It almost caught us. If it had, it would have thrown us back to the shore. Climb in, quick!"

Turn to page 86.

36

You have to duck down in order to get through the door. Since the ceiling is about four feet high, you remain bent over, trying to make yourself as comfortable as possible.

"My name is Thur," he says. "It's actually Thurman Oliver Throckmorton, but you can call me Thur. As you can see, I'm a midget. Oh, don't worry, I'm used to being stared at. I worked in the circus and the movies at one time. When I retired and moved to Gloveville, I had this house built to my own specifications. Campers are really startled when they stumble on my home here in the woods. Children love it, and I love when they visit. It breaks up my time alone here," Thur says, running over to a steaming stove in the corner. He comes back with two bowls of hot cereal. "Now, tell me what happened."

Turn to page 13.

You and Sally decide to go deeper into the cavern. You move silently, keeping as close to the wall as you can. You keep looking for a side passageway that might lead out of the cavern. Finally you see a door set into the wall.

"Do you think we should try it?" Sally asks you.

"Why not? We can't go much farther down this way, or we'll run into those people up ahead."

You go over to the door and listen—you don't hear anything. Then, carefully, you try the handle. Suddenly the door is yanked open from inside, and you stumble through it. A tall figure with a bald head and a long handlebar mustache is standing there, his mouth hanging open in surprise.

"What are you two doing here?" he demands. "You must have somehow gotten away from the bus and—"

You grab Sally's hand and pull her quickly, running farther down the cavern away from him.

"Stop!" the man shouts. Suddenly you see figures running toward you from the other end of the cavern.

Before they reach you, you come to a corridor that intersects with the cavern. Passageways lead away from it on both sides. You have only seconds to decide which direction to take. The passageway to the left leads to a small closed door. The one to the right widens and turns a corner, beyond which you can't see.

If you go to the left, turn to page 89.

If you go to the passageway on the right, turn to page 73.

"I guess you'd better see what they want," you say.

Jason agrees, pulling his car over to the side of the road. The patrol car screeches to a stop behind you. Letters on the side of it say GLOVEVILLE PO-LICE. Two men in uniform jump out with their guns drawn. One of them yanks open the back door of Jason's car. "All right, you two, come out with your hands up," he says.

You and Sally quickly get out.

"Officers, I think you're making a mistake. These kids are trying to escape from some hijackers," Jason explains.

"So that's what they told you, eh?" the man in the uniform says. "If I were you, I'd get out of here fast, before we run you in for aiding fugitives."

Jason sits nervously behind the wheel, not knowing what to do.

"You heard me. Beat it!" the policeman says, slapping the side of Jason's car.

"They're lying!" Sally calls out as Jason drives off. "You saw the newspaper!"

"Shut up, the two of you, and get in the back of the patrol car," the officer says.

Turn to page 50.

The next day, your photo, along with Sally's, is on the front page of every newspaper in the country. The headlines read HIJACKERS CAPTURED. TWO FROM MISSING BUS RESCUED. SEARCH FOR REST OF STUDENTS CONTINUES.

You and Sally lead the rescue mission. It doesn't take long for you to lead the authorities to the terrorists in the caverns and set your classmates free.

The End

You decide to wade across to the opening. You slip down off the ledge into the water. It's ice-cold and makes you gasp for breath. Sally takes your hand as she slips into the stream after you.

"Yikes! It's freezing!" she says.

"This current is really strong. I hope we can make it," you say, starting across. Sally holds on to you. The water is waist deep.

You are about halfway across when you hit a slippery spot and your feet are swept out from under you. The two of you are carried rapidly downstream and into a narrow tunnel. On both sides the walls are high and smooth. There's nothing for you to grab on to.

The stream begins to widen, and you hear a roar up ahead.

"What is that?" Sally asks.

"I . . . don't know," you say. "But . . . it could be a—"

". . . Waterfall! Help!" Sally cries as she tries to swim back against the current. You try to do the same thing—but it's no use. Suddenly you are both swept over the rim of the falls. Fortunately there is only a twenty-foot drop. You plunge several feet under the water and swim back to the surface, sputtering and gasping for air.

Turn to page 96.

"Don't worry. According to my calculations, we should be very close to where we're going by now," Lania says.

"You're right!" you exclaim. "Look, over there. I see something."

"That's it, that's Pine Island," Lania says. "We'll be on the island soon if these currents hold up. Once we get there, I have friends waiting who will help us."

An hour later, you are only about half a mile offshore. "Now row as hard as you can," Lania says.

You and Dan take turns on one oar, while Lania puts all her strength into the other. You are almost to the shore when you hear the sound of a helicopter skimming along the water, coming from the direction of the island you escaped from.

"Is that—" you start.

"It is," Lania says, "but don't give up now, we're almost there."

The helicopter catches up with you and hovers overhead. A man shouts through a megaphone. "Stop rowing at once and let us take you on board. You must come back to the island. You're in no position to refuse."

"What do we do?" Dan asks in a panic. "If we don't go back, they'll kill us."

Go on to the next page.

"If we swim for it, we have a good chance of reaching shore," Lania says.

"They can still catch us in the water," you say. "Maybe we should surrender."

"You decide for yourselves. I'm counting to three and then diving overboard," Lania says. "One, two . . ."

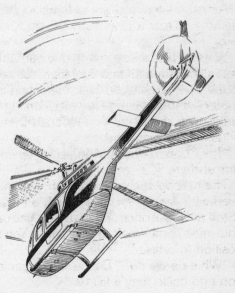

If you decide to swim for the shore, turn to page 71.

If you decide to surrender, turn to page 98.

44

"But you're one of them," you say to Lania.

"This IFF thing is a bunch of nonsense. I believed in it at first, but now I realize how evil and destructive these people are. They don't really care about freedom," she says.

"How can we help you?" you ask. "And why us?"

"I need people I can trust, people who haven't been indoctrinated yet. You two were the first ones who dared to come all the way down to this end of the beach."

"But what do you want us to do?" Dan asks.

"I haven't time for all the details right now, but tonight, after everyone has gone to sleep, sneak out of your dormitory. Go out the back window—someone will be on watch in front. Then come directly here. And *don't* say anything about this to anyone else."

"How will—" you start. But Lania ducks behind the trees and is gone. "What do you make of that?" you ask Dan.

"She could be on the level. It might be worth the risk if it gets us off the island," Dan says.

"It could also be some kind of trick to see if we obey orders," you say. "After all, she *is* part of the hijackers' organization."

If you decide to trust Lania, turn to page 83.

If you decide not to trust her, turn to page 93.

When you wake up, you look around and see lots of sand and palm trees. A group of figures—dressed in the same khaki uniforms as the people in the cavern—are bending over you.

"Where . . where am I?" you ask.

"Welcome to the island headquarters of IFF," one of the men says. "We *know* you will like it here."

The End

"I wish I had something else to cook besides fish. When I get out of here, I'm never going to eat fish again," George says, cooking several small trout over the fire and then handing them to you and Sally.

"This is delicious," Sally says, eating with her fingers off a flat stone in the shape of a dish. You couldn't agree more.

"We're going to rest for a while," Bob says after dinner. "We'll wait for it to get dark before we make our move. Are the two of you coming with us?"

Somehow, you've got to get out of this place, you know. And you might as well try it now. However, the thought that the hijackers may be out there waiting for you gives you reason to pause.

If you try to escape with Bob and his friends, turn to page 82.

If you decide to wait, turn to page 78.

The men go past you, vanishing up the beach. The person on the ground, a young boy, gets up. "I ducked in here when I saw them coming," he says.

"We did the same thing," Dan says.

"Are you two from the new group they just brought in?" he asks.

"Yes," you say. "How about you?"

"My name is Jimmy. I've been here a week," he says. "I was hitchhiking on the mainland when I got a lift from a nice-looking couple. But you never know. As we were riding along, they gave me some soda—or at least I thought it was soda—from a canteen. The next thing I knew, I was on this island. Tonight I'm going to escape."

"We're trying to do the same thing. Do you have a plan?" you ask.

"These people have a small air force—a seaplane, a helicopter, and a transport plane," Jimmy says. "I'm going for the seaplane. I don't think they lock it. They'd never suspect that any of us kids could fly."

"You know how to fly a plane?" you ask.

Go on to the next page.

"Well, my dad taught me how to fly his Cessna," Jimmy says. "I've never actually taken off or landed by myself, though."

"Oh, great," Dan says. "You've never—"

"But I'm sure I can do it. If you two want to come along, you're welcome. If not, good luck."

Should you go with Jimmy? you wonder. You'd sure like to get off the island. But flying with someone who may not know how to take off sounds risky.

If you go with Jimmy, turn to page 102.

If you decide not to, turn to page 104.

The back of the patrol car is like a cage, with a steel grill in front and no door handles on the inside. "How much do you think they told that guy?" you hear the driver say as he heads back toward Gloveville.

"Probably not much, but we'll take the usual precautions," the other officer says.

"You won't get away with this," you holler through the partition. "Jason will report you to the police."

"We *are* the police," the driver says.

"You're also in with the hijackers," you say.

"Keep quiet back there!"

Half an hour later, the squad car arrives back at the police station in Gloveville. The officers drag the two of you out of the car and into the station.

"These two are to be put in solitary. They're to speak with no one—and I mean *no one*," one of the policemen says to another officer inside. "They may look harmless, but they're really mad dogs."

From your windowless cell, you and Sally can only hope that Jason will bring back some police from the next town who will be able to help you.

The End

You and Dan sit there on a damp log, eating the strange fruit. "It's sort of a cross between a lime and a kiwi fruit," he says.

"A kiwi fruit?" you ask.

"Sure, they come from New Zeal—"

Suddenly Dan's eyes get glassy and he seems paralyzed. You try to help him, but you can't move either. The fruit was tasty, no doubt about that, but you were right—it was also deadly!

The End

52

When you wake up, you're in an infirmary. You can tell from the rough stone ceiling that you are back inside the caverns. Your head and leg are bandaged, and you realize suddenly that you are strapped down. A nurse in a white uniform is standing at the foot of your bed, looking at you.

"How are you feeling?" she asks.

"A little dizzy, and my head hurts. Why am I tied to the bed?" you ask.

"Dr. Cranshaw advised it. He said that—oh, here he is now."

You turn your head and see someone coming into the room. It's the man you surprised in the cavern, on the other side of the steel door. With his bald head and handlebar mustache, you'd recognize him anywhere.

"I'm sorry that we had to shoot you in the leg," he says loudly, coming over to the bed and waving the nurse away. "But we couldn't let you get away from us now, could we?"

Go on to the next page.

Dr. Cranshaw examines your bandages and, at the same time, whispers in your ear. "Do exactly as I say, and we both may be able to escape. You're being held by the International Fighters for Freedom. Pretend to join them, and I'll have you assigned to my group. These people are not what I thought they were, they're—"

The nurse comes back, and Dr. Cranshaw straightens up.

"Have you decided to cooperate and join our little operation?" he asks you.

If you trust Dr. Cranshaw and join the IFF, turn to page 6.

If you don't trust him, turn to page 116.

"That'll hold them for a while," the policeman says to himself out loud. "At least until I can get a-hold of Carlos and find out what to do."

An hour later, two more policemen come into the station. You see them down the hallway through the bars. "Remember now, it has to look like suicide," you hear one of them say.

You and Sally crouch in the corner of the cell, wondering what you can do to save yourselves. As the policemen open the door to your cell, you hear police sirens outside, then the screech of brakes. Looking through the bars and down the corridor, you see half a dozen state policemen, their guns drawn, running into the station. They push the three officers against the wall, disarm them, and handcuff their wrists behind their backs at the same time.

"What's going on?" one of the Gloveville officers says. "You can't just come in here like this and arrest us."

"We've had your operation here under surveillance for sometime now," one of the state policemen says. "When we got a call a little over an hour ago from Miss Binnie Atwater at the drugstore telling us that two kids might be in serious danger, we decided to make our move."

Turn to page 39.

You decide to head for the town. "There's a path over there that could lead to a main road," you say.

"The road might be dangerous," Sally says. "What if the hijackers use it to get back and forth from the caverns to the town?"

"We'll be careful. Remember, the hijackers don't even know we escaped from the bus."

Eventually the trail leads to a highway, just as you suspected. There is very little traffic. From the edge of the woods you watch the area. You see a couple of trucks coming in the distance, and you quickly duck behind a tree as they go by. The trucks and their drivers look ordinary enough.

"Let's give the road a try," you say.

Down the road, you come upon a sign that says GLOVEVILLE: 5 MILES. You keep walking.

When you finally reach town, it's almost dark. The streets of Gloveville are strangely deserted, though brightly lit in the twilight.

"Where is everybody?" Sally asks.

"I don't know. All the stores are closed, and it isn't even that late," you say.

The two of you continue up the main street. "There's a drugstore over there that looks like it's open," Sally says.

"Let's try it," you say. You go over and in the front door. There's nobody inside. "Hello? Anybody here?" you call out.

Turn to page 108.

"Let's get out of this town," you say.

"I'm with you," Sally agrees.

The two of you hurry along, turning onto a side street. Then, after a few blocks, you turn left and head for the other side of town. You keep walking, passing the last houses of the town before returning to the main highway. A road sign ahead says that it's thirty-five miles to Denver.

You've been hiking at a brisk pace for a while when you see the flashing lights of a police car coming in your direction. "Quick!" you say. "Over behind those trees."

You watch as the patrol car passes by. It goes down the road a mile or so, then makes a U-turn and comes back slowly, heading in the direction of Gloveville. When the car is out of sight again, you and Sally start off, keeping a careful lookout behind you. In the next two hours, the police car passes by several times. You manage to hide each time.

Sometime later, you see a pair of headlights coming from the direction of Gloveville. You are about to run for cover when you realize that it's a truck. "Do you think we should try to hitch a ride?" you say.

"Why not?" Sally says. "My feet are killing me."

You hold out your thumb as the truck gets closer. Its air brakes hiss as it slows to a stop. "Can you give us a lift?" you call up to the driver.

"Jump in the back," he calls down.

Turn to page 19.

Suddenly the door behind you slams shut. You run over to it and try to open it. "Now this one is locked too. We're trapped in between," you say.

At the same time, water starts rising up around your ankles. Soon it's up to your knees.

"This chamber is going to be completely filled with water in a few minutes!" Sally exclaims. "We have to get out of here!"

You throw all your weight against one door—and then against the other, but it's no use. The water keeps rising until it's up to the ceiling. When the water eventually goes down again, it leaves two lifeless bodies on the floor of the chamber.

The End

"Let's try to get past the guard," you say.

You and Sally tiptoe out of your hiding place and head toward the guard. As you get closer, you can see that he's definitely asleep—and snoring. You hug the wall opposite him as you go by. The guard stirs restlessly for a moment, but he doesn't wake up.

You get past him and look cautiously around a bend in the cavern wall. You push Sally back—there are two more guards standing next to what looks like a door leading to the outside.

"More guards," you whisper to Sally.

"Does this mean we'll have to go back?" she whispers.

You nod. But just as you start back, the guard wakes up and yawns. He doesn't seem to notice you.

On the other side of the cavern, not far from the guard who just woke up, there's a small door cut into the wall. You point to it, afraid to make a sound.

Your heart skips a beat as the guard gets up. He still doesn't notice you and Sally. Then he turns and looks the other way. You grab Sally's hand, and the two of you move—as quietly as you can—across the floor of the cavern.

Turn to page 12.

The two FBI men sneak you and Sally out the back of the police station. A van is waiting to take you to the farm. You and Sally get into the back, and the FBI men close the door. Suddenly you realize that the two men who are supposed to protect you are both tied up and gagged. You turn around to try to get out of the van, but a dark hood is pulled over your head, and your hands are tied behind your back. As the van drives away, the heavy smell of chloroform hits you. Before you lose consciousness, you hear someone say, "We'll take the kids to our new location." But that's the last you hear.

The End

"Let's make a run for it," you say to Jason.

"I've always wanted to try this," he says, flooring the gas pedal. The car leaps forward.

The patrol car starts after you, its siren wailing. You look out the back window. "Look, they're going as fast as they can," you say, "but they're falling way behind."

Jason goes around a wide curve at top speed and then climbs a long, steep hill. Up ahead is a tractor-trailer hogging your side of the road. Traffic is coming past it from the other direction.

"If we get stuck behind that trailer, the patrol car will surely catch up with us," you say.

"Right. Our only hope is to get past it," Jason says, slowing the car down when it reaches the truck.

The patrol car is coming fast, and the man on the passenger side has his arm out the window. He's aiming a gun in your direction.

You are thrown against the door as Jason swerves out into the other lane and floors the accelerator. The car shoots past the truck and back into your lane.

"We were lucky for that break," Jason says. "With this stream of traffic coming up ahead now, I'd like to see that patrol car try to pass that truck."

Turn to page 70.

64

"You're right," you say. "We don't even know who that man is. Let's stay hidden for a while."

You and Sally go back through the woods to the small clearing that you passed earlier. Both of you slump down, slowly drifting off to sleep.

Hours later, you wake up. The light of the moon has been replaced by the pale gray of early dawn. You get up and stretch, stiff from sleeping on the ground. Sally is still asleep. You shake her gently. She wakes up with a start.

"What I'd like most now—after a good breakfast, of course—is a hot shower," Sally says. "I feel itchy after sleeping all night on the ground."

"The main thing is to get as far away from the hijackers as we can. There's a path going off to the side. It should go around the campers or whoever they are."

"All right, let's go," Sally says. "Maybe we'll find a stream where we can wash up."

The two of you start out.

"Look at the way the tree branches arch low overhead," you say. "This path is almost like a tunnel."

"A tunnel for midgets, perhaps," Sally says, walking with her head bent down. "Or for some kind of animal."

Go on to the next page.

"If animals made this path, they also lined up small paving stones to mark the way. They'd have to be pretty clever to do that," you say.

You continue to walk on for a while. "I'm getting pretty tired of walking bent over," Sally says. "Maybe we can find a different trail."

"Let's go just a bit farther. I have a feeling that—" you begin to say, but the sight up ahead stops you in mid sentence.

Turn to page 29.

You and Sally follow Thur through the trapdoor and down a ladder to the underground passageway. Thur brings along a lantern to light the way. Soon you begin to hear shouting. You stop. "I don't think we should go any farther," Sally says.

"Don't be afraid," Thur says. "We'll be able to see them, but they won't be able to see us. Relax, I've watched them many times."

"All right," you say.

The three of you start forward again. The shouting gets louder as you come to a dead end in the tunnel—or almost a dead end. There are several holes in the wall. The sound is coming out of one of them.

"Look through here," Thur says. "But be careful not to stick your head in too far. You don't want anyone to see you."

You look through one of the holes and see a vast cavern filled with hundreds of figures, all wearing khaki uniforms. A figure is standing in front of them with his arm upraised. The shouting of the crowd stops as he lowers his hand and starts to speak. Even though he is far below, his voice carries to your lookout point.

"We of the International Fighters for Freedom must show no mercy to the enemies of the revolution. They must be eliminated . . ."

Suddenly you hear the sound of footsteps running toward you in the tunnel.

Turn to page 92.

For a short time, the road you're traveling on in the darkness is bumpy. Then, after a sharp turn, it gets smooth once again. "I'll bet we're back on the main highway," you say. "It feels like we're going really fast."

"Maybe the police will stop the van and give the driver a ticket for speeding," Sally says hopefully.

"Even if they do, they won't necessarily ask to look inside the van."

"What do you think this hijacking is all about?" Sally asks.

"I don't know. I just hope they're not terrorists," you speculate. You feel the van start to climb steadily uphill.

"What do you think they'll do if they catch us in here?"

"I'm trying not to think about it," you say. "Let's go back and take a look out that crack in the door. Maybe we can figure out where we are."

"We're going through some town," Sally says. "I saw a store with the name GLOVEVILLE HARD-WARE on it."

You take a turn at the crack.

"We were. Now we're past the town and in the country," you say.

Turn to page 76.

68

You manage to unlock the latch and push the trapdoor open. You squeeze yourself up through it and signal for Sally to follow.

You find yourself inside a pipe, just large enough to crawl through on all fours. You feel a strong rush of air.

Sally is soon behind you. "This is awful," she says. "I'm really claustrophobic. I hate tight places like this. Suppose we get trapped at the other end."

"This could be a vent to pipe in fresh air," you say. "If it is, it should lead to the outside. It could also be an emergency escape route from the caverns. Either way, let's hurry up and get out of here."

A faint light, you notice, is coming from one end of the tube. You and Sally crawl toward it. When you get to where the tube makes a right angle, you go straight up. Another ladder leads to the top.

"I see a metal grating up there," you say. "If we're lucky, it'll have a latch on this side just as the trapdoor did."

You climb up the ladder. You are right, the grate does have a latch on the inside. You unlock it, push it open, and climb out. Sally follows right behind you.

For a moment the two of you stand there, gazing around in amazement.

Turn to page 16.

70

Jason pours on the gas, and you go streaking down the highway. A sign warns SPEED ZONE AHEAD. A little farther on, another sign says DENVER SPEED LIMIT: 30 MPH.

Suddenly a Denver patrol car pulls out from behind a billboard. With its siren going, it too starts after you!

"We'll stop and explain why we're going so fast," Jason says, pulling over to the side of the highway. The police car pulls up behind.

Turn to page 27.

". . . Three," Lania calls out as she dives overboard. You and Dan join her, diving off the other end of the boat, going deep under the water.

You breaststroke and hold your breath as long as you can. You come up for air at the same time as Dan. For a moment, you hear the rat-tat-tat of a machine gun, and you both take a big gulp of air and dive back down.

Suddenly the bottom rises up from below you, and you find yourself in shallow water. You stand up, the water coming up to your knees. Dan surfaces not too far away. You hear the sound of the helicopter overhead. There are dozens of other bathers around you, all dashing out of the water and running for safety. The man in the helicopter can't fire at you without hitting the others. It turns around and swerves away.

Turn to page 110.

You and Sally dash down the corridor to the right. You go around the curve and come to a wide double door. You go through it and find yourselves in an immense underground amphitheater. Hundreds of figures dressed in makeshift khaki uniforms are lined up in rows on both sides of a central aisle. As all eyes turn to look at you, you and Sally stand there for a few moments, not knowing what to do. A loud murmur goes through the crowd.

"Silence!" a figure in a somewhat more elaborate uniform at the far end of the aisle commands. "Bring them forward."

The guards from the outside corridor grab the two of you and escort you down the aisle to where their leader stands in front of a huge pit. The other figures gather around you.

"Now you will see what happens to those who oppose us!" he screams.

You and Sally are tossed over the edge of the pit, hurtling down into the abyss. By the time you hit bottom, you don't feel a thing.

The End

"I don't think we should go back to the caverns for *any* reason," you say. "I think it's time for us to move on."

You thank Thur for his kindness, and he takes you to a trail leading to the highway a few miles away. "Don't trust the police in Gloveville," he says. "Some of them are in cahoots with the cavern people."

You thank Thur once again and start out through the woods. As promised, the trail comes out on the side of the highway. You are at the top of a hill. The road drops steeply away in both directions. A nearby sign says GLOVEVILLE: 5 MILES.

"Which way should we go?" Sally asks.

"Thur warned us about the police in Gloveville," you say.

"But going through town is the shortest way back home," Sally says. "We don't even know where the highway leads to in the other direction."

"You're right," you say. "But it might be safer to do as Thur said and avoid the town."

*If you decide to go toward Gloveville,
turn to page 111.*

*If you decide to go in the opposite direction,
turn to page 115.*

You watch as Sally slips under the bus. Then you and Dan do as you've been told and go outside.

"All right, you two, get in line!" one of the masked men shouts.

Behind you, they drag Buzzy out of the bus and into a car off to the side. When they open the door to push him in, you get a glimpse of Mrs. Wilson inside, gagged and tied, her hands behind her back.

A truck then backs up into position in front of you and your fellow classmates. "All right, everyone inside!" one of the hijackers says. The truck has a bench seat running around the inside. You get in and sit down with the others. It's a tight squeeze.

The door slams shut, and the truck starts off. It travels along a bumpy road for about half an hour, then comes to a sudden stop.

Everyone is unloaded, and you find yourself at the side of a broad field, next to a large airplane. It looks like an army transport, except that it has no markings.

You board the plane, and it takes off immediately. Your seat is next to a window. However, the window is covered over—as are all the others—with a black curtain so that you can't see out.

Turn to page 21.

A short time later, the van turns off onto a rough side road. The thin crack of light turns into darkness. "Hey!" you exclaim. "We just entered a tunnel, or maybe a cave."

The van comes to a stop. "We'd better hide inside the bus in case somebody opens the back," you whisper.

You run back into the bus and duck down just as the door of the van is lowered.

Turn to page 7.

You and Sally start upstream along the ledge. As you go, it gets narrower and narrower, until it's barely wide enough to walk on.

"Looks like we're going to have to go back," Sally says.

"I don't think so," you say. "Look, right up ahead, there's a steel door fitted into the wall. If we can get to it, maybe it's open."

The ledge is now only an inch or so wide. Your foot keeps slipping off. You cling to the wall and slowly work your way forward. You've made it. As best you can, you push on the door. It swings open easily. With your last ounce of strength, you grab the edge of the doorframe and pull yourself through. Then you help Sally climb in.

You find yourself in a narrow chamber, on the other side of which is another iron door. You go over and push on it, but it won't budge.

"There doesn't seem to be a latch on this side. I hope that—" you start to say.

Turn to page 58.

You decide to stay in the cave and wait. You watch as the group led by Bob scales the stone wall and vanishes into the pale moonlight high above.

A few minutes later, you hear gunshots and screams from the outside, then silence.

"I hope some of them managed to escape," Sally says.

"I'm sure they did," you say. "They'll go and send help. I'll bet we're rescued soon."

You are rescued, but it's not anytime soon. It's a few months before a voice calls from above. "Hello. Is anyone down there?"

"Yes, we're here," you call back. "Help us."

A rope ladder comes tumbling down, and all of you climb up one at a time. You and Sally are the first to go.

Several tall men in trench coats and broad-rimmed hats are standing at the top. "My name is Agent Mitchell from the FBI," one of them says. "It took us a while, but we finally found you. The rest of your classmates were rescued a few weeks ago. They led us to the caverns, and we've been able to break apart the terrorist organization."

"You got here just in time," you say. "I don't think I could have eaten another one of those fish."

The End

You get up early the next morning. The sky is gray and drizzly. Jason is already awake, and you and Sally help him take down the tent and load it into the trunk of the car.

"This is a beautiful car," you say.

"Thanks," Jason says. "It has a supercharged V–8 engine. It's a lot more power than I need, but I like the idea of it being there. Might come in handy someday. You never can tell."

You walk down to a nearby stream and splash cold water on your face while Jason finishes packing up his fishing gear.

"You're sure you don't want to go to the police in Gloveville?" Jason asks when you get back.

"Someone else may have escaped from the hijackers last night," you say. "We're not *sure,* but if anyone did, then the hijackers may be on the lookout in town."

"Don't worry," Jason says. "To the people in town, you two are my children."

You and Sally climb into the car, and Jason heads off, driving along an old logging road through the woods. Soon you are on the main highway going toward Gloveville.

Several police cars go by. As they do, they slow down and take a long, careful look. Just before you enter town, you are stopped by a police roadblock. A man in uniform comes up to the car and looks all of you over.

Turn to page 24.

"I don't think it's going to be so easy to escape," you say. "But let's walk along the beach. Maybe we'll think of something."

You and Dan go down to the far end of the beach and sit down on the sand under a grove of palm trees near the rope.

"We could jump over the rope and head farther up the beach," Dan says. "Maybe we can—"

"Not a chance," you say. "The hijackers will just catch us and bring us back—after all, we're on an island."

"I guess you're right."

You're looking out over the ocean when you hear a low "pssst" come from the direction of the trees. You look around. At first you don't see her, then you do—it's Lania, peeking around a tree and beckoning you with her finger.

You and Dan step over the rope and head toward the trees. "Quick, duck down," Lania says, reaching out and pulling the two of you into the grove. "This is dangerous for me too," she says, "but I need your help. We've got to get off this island. With your help, we can escape."

Turn to page 44.

"I'm with you," you tell Bob, looking at Sally for her decision.

"Count me in," she says.

"You know, it might be better if you stay here," you tell her. "There's no point in both of us taking a chance. If I get away, I'll go to the police and come back for you, I promise."

"All right," Sally says. "But you'd better not forget about me."

That night, once it's dark and a pale shaft of moonlight shines down through the cavern opening, you say good-bye to Sally and the others, promising to get help. You start out with Bob, a boy named Darcey, and Norma. Bob leads the way. When your turn comes, you brace yourself in a wide crack in the cavern wall. While sliding your back up against the stone, you manage to push yourself up with your feet.

As you get near the top, your muscles ache and your back hurts. For a moment you're not sure if you will make it, but you grit your teeth and give it a final push.

Turn to page 94.

"I think we should trust her," you say.

"I do too," Dan says.

That evening, Lania returns to lead everyone to the dining tent for supper. Several guards hover nearby, but they don't bother anyone. You realize that they won't do anything as long as everyone behaves the way they're supposed to and follows orders.

The rest of the evening is spent watching television. Instead of commercials, there are several minutes of flashing lights between the programs. These flashes make you slightly dizzy, but somehow you can't tear your eyes away from them. You wonder if they are part of the brainwashing.

When it's time to go to bed, you have to fight to stay awake—you keep seeing the flashing lights from the television—they seem to hypnotize you. You manage to lie awake, pretending to sleep.

You wait for a while. As soon as all the others are fast asleep, you carefully get up and tiptoe over to Dan's bunk. He is ready to go. The two of you climb outside through a back window as quietly as you can. You stand there listening. All is quiet, except for the sound of surf not far away.

Then you creep around to the back of the building, getting clear of it before starting toward the beach. The night is cloudy, but the sky is luminous enough for you to make out where you are going.

Soon you are on the beach where you talked to Lania earlier in the day. "I'm over here," she whispers. "Follow me." You're so nervous, she startles you.

Turn to page 35.

84

Soon you reach a small clearing. "This looks like a good place to camp," you say. You and Sally both slump down on the ground with your backs against a tree. The moonlight throws long shadows through the branches all around you.

"It's probably my imagination," Sally says, "but I could swear that I smell something cooking."

"I smell it too," you say. "It seems to be coming from that direction. It could be coming from a house, or a campsite. I don't know about you, but I'm starved. That looks like a path going in the right direction. Let's follow it."

"All right, but let's be careful. Those hijackers could also be patrolling the woods."

You and Sally slowly walk along the path. Soon you see a flickering yellow light through the trees. "It's a campfire," you whisper to Sally. A man is sitting next to it, roasting marshmallows. "Do you think he'd give us some food?"

"Food? Forget about food. He could be in with the hijackers."

"That's true. But he could also be someone just camping out in the woods."

Would it be wise to reveal yourselves at this point? you wonder. Or should you stay hidden in the woods for the time being?

If you decide to reveal yourselves, turn to page 22.

If you decide to stay hidden, turn to page 64.

The three of you pull yourselves up over the side of the boat and tumble inside. "Grab this," Lania says, handing you an oar. "It fits in the oarlock over there." She gives another oar to Dan. "Now row," she says, as she starts bailing out the boat with a large pail.

You and Dan dig into the water with your oars. Luckily you both learned how to row on Clover Lake back home.

"We're doing well," Lania says, as you pull away from the island. "The currents are offshore tonight. They should carry us out to sea. If we're lucky, the weather reports will be right, and we'll be in a fog bank by morning."

"That's lucky?" you say.

"When they discover that we're gone," Lania says, "they'll be out looking for us. They have a helicopter. The last time someone tried to escape, they caught them from the air."

"How far do we have to go before we're safe?" Dan asks.

"There are islands to the north. I've charted a route with the prevailing currents helping us. If we take turns rowing all night and part of the morning, we should reach them by noon tomorrow. There's three of us. Two can rest while the other rows. I brought along some fruit and a canteen of water for each of us."

"Let's just hope we don't all get tired at the same time," Dan says.

Go on to the next page.

You and Dan row for an hour, then Lania takes over for you for a while, then you take over for Dan. Lania seems tireless, periodically checking her compass and a chart using a penlight.

Toward morning, the sky begins to lighten. Sure enough, the fog rolls over you, just as Lania predicted. "This is great," she says. "They'll never be able to find us in this."

Less than an hour later, the fog starts to lift. "I think we're in trouble," Dan says.

Turn to page 42.

The Gloveville men look at each other for a few seconds, trying to decide what to do. Reluctantly they get back into their patrol car and speed off.

"You're just going to let them go like that?" you say in amazement.

"Don't worry, we'll contact the Colorado state police and have them picked up," the Denver officer says. "Right now, follow our patrol car back to the station. We'll radio ahead to the FBI and have them bring over their file on the hijacking."

Jason pulls up in front of the police station and parks right behind the patrol car. The two Denver policemen escort the three of you inside. The file on the hijacking is there and school pictures of you and Sally from the year before. You haven't changed that much.

The Denver police drop the speeding charges on Jason. In fact, they thank him for helping to rescue you.

Two FBI agents spend the next two hours questioning you. You tell them everything you know as best you can. Unfortunately, they're not quite convinced. They keep questioning you, trying to break your story. Meanwhile, a detachment of Colorado state police is sent to raid the caverns outside Gloveville, and the newspapers and your families are told of your rescue. The police station is besieged by reporters.

Later, negative reports come back about the raid on the caverns. As far as the Colorado police can determine, they were boarded up twenty years ago for safety reasons.

Turn to page 30.

"This way—to the left," you tell Sally.

Quickly you head for the small door. Your pursuers are not far behind. "Don't let them get away!" one of them shouts.

A heavy padlock is hanging on the latch. Fortunately it's not locked. You pull it off and hand it to Sally as you push the steel door open and squeeze through.

"We're in luck. There's another latch on this side," you say. "Quick, close the door and lock it with the padlock."

Sally slams the door and locks it, seconds before your pursuers get there. Angry shouts come from the other side. "Why was this door left unlocked?" someone demands. "Get a crew and break it down."

"It's really dark in here," Sally says, as you turn around and slowly start through a narrow passageway.

"We'll just keep going as best we can and see where this leads. Maybe it's a way out of the caverns," you say, trying to sound optimistic.

Turn to page 100.

A young woman with long blond hair comes out from behind a grove of palm trees and over to your group. She is wearing a normal dress, but it's the same khaki color as the fatigues worn by the others. She waves the guard away.

"My name is Lania. Welcome to the island headquarters of the International Fighters for Freedom," she says. "You've been liberated from your school and families where you have been taught lies about life. There are many groups of us around the world and in your own country. I will tell you more in the days ahead, but first I'm sure you would all like some refreshments. So, if you will follow me . . ."

Lania leads your group through the grove of palm trees and over to a large tent. Inside, several low circular tables are piled with desserts. Everyone sits cross-legged on the blanket that covers the floor and starts to eat.

"This is great—just like summer camp," one of your classmates says. "I hope it keeps up this way."

You have to admit that the food is pretty good. Dan especially is enjoying himself. "This is what I call being kidnapped in style," he says.

"I don't know," you say. "It depends on the price we have to pay for it."

"Price?" Dan asks.

"I mean, what we'll be expected to do in return, and what they'll do to us later if we don't."

Turn to page 26.

"We've been discovered! Quick, through here!" Thur exclaims.

He disappears into a small, semicircular opening cut into the base of the side wall. Sally follows him on her hands and knees, with you right behind her. You are halfway through the opening when someone grabs your ankle and drags you back out. In seconds several men have your hands and feet tied and are carrying you off. It's the last you see of Sally and the strange midget named Thur.

The End

That night, after everyone is asleep, you and Dan sneak out of the barracks. Instead of going to the meeting place with Lania, the two of you go in the opposite direction.

"Where are we going?" Dan whispers.

"I'm not sure," you whisper back. "But anything is better than what I'm afraid the IFF people have in store for us."

"Do you think we should tell Lania first?" Dan asks.

"I don't really trust her," you say. "That's why we're going the other way."

You leave the area of the dormitory, coming out on the beach well beyond the rope fence. You and Dan head down the beach, keeping close to the palm trees that run along the land side. Then, up ahead, you see some figures with flashlights coming in your direction. Quickly, you duck behind the nearest tree and step on something soft on the ground. You hear a groan.

"I think I just stepped on somebody," you whisper to Dan.

"You did," a voice whispers from the ground. "Right on my foot."

"Who are you?" Dan asks.

"Don't either of you say anything until the beach patrol goes by," the voice whispers. "They make hourly checks at this time of night."

The three of you remain silent in the shadows as several men crunch by in the sand. You hear the crackle of their walkie-talkies above the sound of the surf.

Turn to page 48.

94

Somehow you manage to reach the top. You lie there for a few moments, shaking with fright, realizing what you have just done. One slip and you could have fallen fifty feet to the bottom of the shaft. Slowly you get to your feet and climb up the jumble of rocks that leads out of the cavern. Looking out over a wide expanse of landscape, you see the lights of a town twinkle in the distance. In the other direction is a high, rocky hill.

Suddenly a beam of light stabs down from above. "It's the hijackers!" Bob hollers up ahead. "Scatter, everyone go a different way. They can't catch all of us."

You start to run down the slope in front of you, but the beam of light catches you. There is the sharp crack of a rifle shot from behind, and you feel a stab of pain in your leg as you sprawl to the ground. Your head hits something hard, and everything goes black.

Turn to page 52.

You manage to tread water for a few minutes, looking around the wide pool that you've fallen into. There's a beach on the far side, and you and Sally swim over to it. Looking up, you see a patch of blue sky high overhead. The beach slopes up to a jumble of large boulders. Beyond that, a sheer rock wall rises to the opening above.

"That's our way out," you say, pointing to the opening. "If we can figure a way to get up there."

Suddenly a young but gaunt face appears from behind one of the boulders, then vanishes again.

"What the—. Hello? Who are you?" you call out.

A boy about your own age comes out from behind the rocks. "We escaped from some hijackers," he says as he comes over to you. "My name's Bob."

"We escaped from the hijackers too," you say.

Bob turns back toward the boulders and whistles. A group of kids, boys and girls, come out from behind the rocks. "We haven't been able to escape from this cavern," Bob says. "We've more or less figured out how to scale the walls, but they have guards posted outside. Some of us have been trapped here for months. A few have tried to escape, but they were captured."

Go on to the next page.

"What do you eat?" Sally asks.

"It's easy to spear small fish here in the shallows," Bob says. "One of us, George, is a Boy Scout. He knows how to start a fire so that we can cook them. We don't really have much of a choice. Some of us are going to make an escape attempt tonight. You're welcome to come along. We can only hope the hijackers won't get us. But first, come, let's get something to eat."

Turn to page 33.

". . . Three!" Lania shouts as she dives overboard. You and Dan remain in the boat, waving your arms in surrender. Suddenly bullets start to spatter the surface of the ocean all around the spot where Lania went under. The helicopter circles around your boat, firing at different areas. You hope that Lania got away. You haven't seen her surface since she dived overboard.

The helicopter comes back and hovers directly over your boat. The men aboard send down a rope ladder, and you and Dan climb up. Then the copter goes straight up about a thousand feet.

The men aboard look at each other and smile. "It's time for your diving lessons," one of them says.

"What do you mean by that?" you say.

"Just this," he says as he pushes you and Dan out of the open door of the helicopter.

The End

100

After a while, the passageway begins to widen, and you come out into another cavern. It's almost completely filled with a wide, underground stream. A narrow ledge runs along the side you are on, leading upstream just above the swiftly flowing water. The cavern ceiling, arching high overhead, is broken by a ragged opening through which a hazy shaft of daylight shines down. Directly across the stream you see a doorlike opening in the cavern wall.

"The water doesn't look deep," Sally says. "I can see the bottom. We can either wade across to that opening or follow the ledge. Once they get through that door they'll be coming after us again."

Wading across might be risky, you think. The bottom might be slippery, or there could be sinkholes. On the other hand, the ledge could lead to a dead end.

If you go upstream along the ledge, turn to page 77.

If you try wading across to the opening, turn to page 40.

You and Sally dash into the administration building at once. A man is standing there by the watercooler. "Do you know where I can find Smitty?" you ask him.

"That's me," the man says.

You hand him the note from the truck driver.

"Why sure, I'd be glad to—" he starts.

"Right now, there's a bigger problem," Sally says. "Two people we know are being kidnapped outside."

"Kidnapped? Are you sure? I thought something was fishy with those two men out there," Smitty says, opening a desk drawer and taking out a revolver. "Wait right here."

He runs out, bringing back the kidnappers at gunpoint. Mrs. Wilson and Buzzy Hargrove are smiling broadly. They sure are glad to see you and Sally.

"Now I'll call the police," Smitty says, picking up the phone. "I'm still not sure what this is all about."

"It's all part of a school bus hijacking," Sally says.

"The one on the news!?" Smitty exclaims.

"That's right," you say. "And I'm sure the news has reported only half of it. Just wait. Have we got a story to tell."

The End

"We'll go with you," you say. "We have to try something."

"Good," Jimmy says. "You two will come in handy. They have a constant guard in front of the seaplane. That's why I'm thinking they keep it ready to take off at any time. Now here's my plan—the guard stands right at the end of the pier. If one of you can push him off into the water, I'll be able to cut the lines and get the plane warmed up. We should have enough time to take off before they can stop us."

"Oh, great," Dan says. "You take off while we're left holding the bag."

"Come on! I wouldn't do that. Trust me."

"All right," you say hesitantly. "But I don't know about this."

"Don't worry. Follow me, and be careful. We have to be quiet and stick to the shadows."

You and Dan follow Jimmy along the beach, then head inland. He seems to know where he's going. Soon you see the lagoon and the seaplane up ahead, barely visible in the dim light.

The three of you creep to the base of the pier. You see a brief flash of light as the guard lights a cigarette. You take off your sneakers and slowly creep down the pier. The guard hears something and turns toward you at the last moment, but he's too late. You rush forward and give him a shove, sending him flying over the edge. As he does, his finger pulls back on the trigger of his machine gun. A burst of gunfire shatters the silence. Then you hear a splash, and the firing stops.

Turn to page 112.

"I'm afraid it sounds too risky," you say.

"All right, I'll go by myself," Jimmy says. "I understand. And to show you that there's no hard feelings, I'll help you out. Go all the way down the beach to the end of the island. There's a jungle area there. When I get to the mainland, I'll tell the police. You can hide there and wait."

"That's really nice of you," you say. "Good luck."

"Thanks. Good luck yourselves," Jimmy says, slipping off into the darkness.

Keeping close to the water so that the surf will wipe out your footprints, you and Dan start your hike down the beach. Sometime later, you hear the sound of guns firing far behind you, then the sound of a seaplane. You hope Jimmy made it.

It is already faintly light out by the time you get to the end of the island. "Jimmy was right," you say. "Inland it's all jungle here."

"Do you think it's safe to hide in there?" Dan asks.

"A lot safer than out in the open here on the beach," you say. "We can go just inside the trees."

Turn to page 17.

"Let's head for the woods," you say. "We can hide out there until tomorrow morning, then decide what to do next. It should be dark soon. We'll make our move at twilight, when we can still see where we're going but it's difficult for anyone to spot us."

An hour later, the last rays of the sun fan out over the sky like fiery searchlights. "The sunset is beautiful," Sally says.

"It is," you say. "Let's get ready. It's almost time to start—" You break off.

"What's the matter?" Sally asks.

"Down there, at the entrance to the cavern. I just saw two men come out and go partway down the road." You hear the crackle of walkie-talkies.

"Do you think we've been spotted?" Sally says.

"No, I don't think so," you say. "They would have come directly toward us. It could be a routine patrol."

Sure enough, after a while, the men go back into the cavern. You and Sally decide it's time to slip out of your hiding place and head toward the woods. The last sparks of the sunset are dying out, and a bright moon is rising on the opposite horizon.

You are almost to the woods when a beam of light cuts across the field behind you.

Turn to page 20.

"What are we going to do?" Dan asks.

"One of these switches on the control panel is supposed to send out an emergency signal to the U.S. Coast Guard," Dan says. "But I'm not sure which one. I didn't pay too much attention when my father was showing me."

"What about this one here?" you say, pointing to a knob on the control panel. "I'll bet—"

"I don't know, but let's try it," Jimmy says, pulling the knob.

You feel a sharp jar inside the plane, and something whooshes from underneath. Suddenly a huge ball of flame erupts in front of you. Jimmy veers the plane off to the side to miss it.

"Wow!" Jimmy exclaims. "We just eliminated our unfriendly local helicopter. I think this plane was equipped with an air-to-air missile."

"Jimmy, when we get home, we're going to throw one heck of a party for you," you say.

When you get to the mainland, you tell the authorities about the island. They quickly dispatch a Coast Guard ship and storm ashore, rescuing the other kids who were hijacked. The terrorists are arrested and brought back to the mainland to stand trial.

The End

You wait at the front door for a while. You're about to leave when an old woman comes out of the back. "Yes, can I help you?" she asks.

"I'd like to know—" you start.

"You're strangers in town, aren't you?" she interrupts. "Visiting somebody?"

"We're looking for the police station," Sally says.

"The police station is two blocks down that way," she says, pointing. "I don't know what you want there, but I'd avoid it if I was you. The town police are . . . well, not very helpful around here."

"Thanks," you say, going out the door. Hesitantly you and Sally turn around and walk up the street toward the police station.

"Could some of the police really be involved in the hijacking?" you say. "It doesn't seem likely. Maybe the two men we saw in the caverns were just masquerading as policemen."

"You heard what that woman said about them," Sally says. "Maybe we should get to the other side of town by a side street and avoid the police station."

If you go to the police station, turn to page 10.

If you take a side street to the other side of town, turn to page 57.

You decide to stay where you are. You continue to lie there in the hot sun near the shore all day and throughout the night. The following morning Dan says, "I'm going back. I don't care what they do to me. It can't be as bad as starving to death out here."

"All right," you say. "Let's go back. I guess Jimmy didn't make it."

It takes you most of the day to hike back. As you get close to the IFF camp, you see men in uniforms carrying rifles running up and down the beach. They are rounding up the hijackers. Then you see Jimmy.

"Hey," he calls over, "I was just going to come and look for you. I just landed with the Coast Guard."

"You made it!" you say, running over and shaking his hand.

You're free, and before long you are sitting with your family eating a nice homemade meal, telling them everything that happened. You can hardly believe it yourself.

The End

Lania comes ashore farther down the beach. She has a gash in her arm where a bullet has grazed her. A lifeguard helps her toward the first aid station. You and Dan follow, trailing behind.

"That was close!" Lania says. "Now let's find my friends. Then we'll tell our story to the local police."

The End

You and Sally decide to walk toward Gloveville. After a few minutes you see a car in the distance coming toward town.

"Is it a police car?" Sally asks.

"No . . . it's just an ordinary car. A couple of people inside."

"Let's take a chance," Sally says. "Maybe they're going to the next town after Gloveville."

The two of you stand on the side of the road with your thumbs out. The car comes to a stop. Inside are a middle-aged man in a business suit and a woman—his wife, you guess—wearing a print dress. "Jump in the back," the man says.

You and Sally get in, and the car starts off again. "We're going to Denver," the driver says.

"Oh, great. That's where we're going too," you say.

You look nervously out the window as the car goes through Gloveville, but you are soon on the other side of town.

"You kids must be thirsty from being out on the road," the woman says, handing you back a thermos bottle. "Here's some lemonade. You can finish it off if you like."

You and Sally both take a few big gulps. Soon you start to feel dizzy, and everything looks blurred.

Turn to page 45.

Lights go on in a nearby building, and shouts come from somewhere next to it. Jimmy has already cut the lines mooring the plane and is inside. "Jump in, quick!" he shouts.

You and Dan dive through the door as the propeller starts to turn. In a few seconds, Jimmy has it revved up, and the plane is heading out into the lagoon.

"We did it!" he shouts as the plane leaves the surface of the water and rises into the air. "This thing has a full tank of gas. We're on our way."

"Do you know which way to go?" you ask.

"My father taught me how to use the flight compass. I'm pretty sure the mainland is north-northwest. It shouldn't take us long to get there—an hour maybe."

You've been flying for about ten minutes when a helicopter appears, flying alongside you.

The plane's radio starts to crackle, then a voice comes on: "Attention seaplane. Go back to the island at once or we'll be forced to shoot you down. You have thirty seconds to comply."

Turn to page 107.

"All right, everyone out," one of the masked men orders, untying Mrs. Wilson's hands from the steering wheel and pushing her ahead of him through the door of the bus. There is just enough room between the side of the bus and the inside of the van for you and your classmates to leave in single file. One by one everyone on the bus starts out. One of the gunmen stands inside the bus and another stands just outside the door, making sure no one gets away.

You, Sally, and Dan are last to get out. You are off the bus and working your way to the back of the van when you hear Buzzy Hargrove. He's still in the bus, freaking out, screaming, "Don't touch me! Don't touch me!" He must have been hiding under one of the seats, you realize.

While the first gunman is pulling him out, the other gunman jumps aboard to help. For a few seconds, you, Sally, and Dan are left alone in the space between the bus and the van.

"Let's hide under the bus," Sally whispers. "Who knows what they're going to do to us when we leave here."

"It won't work," Dan says. "They'll just find us and pull us out, like they're doing to Buzzy."

"I'm going to try it anyway," Sally says.

Whatever your decision, you're going to have to make it fast.

If you decide to do as you've been told by the hijackers, turn to page 75.

If you hide under the bus with Sally, turn to page 4.

You and Sally hike in the opposite direction, away from Gloveville. A few cars go past, heading for the town, but none pass in your direction. Finally, an hour later, a truck lumbers up the road behind you. The driver sees you and stops.

"You two want a lift?" he calls down.

"Sure do," you say, climbing inside.

"How far you going?" the driver asks as he starts up again.

"We're not sure," Sally says. "We're trying to get to the city."

"You're going in the wrong direction, then," the driver says. "Want me to stop and let you out?"

"No, that's okay. We'll go wherever you're going," Sally says.

"That's a long trip," the driver says. "I'll tell you what. There's a small airport a few miles ahead. I know the guy, Smitty, who runs it. He flies to the city at least twice a day. Give him my name, and maybe he'll take you with him. In fact, here, I'll write you a note."

When you get to the airport, you thank the driver. Then you walk over toward the small administration building. Several small planes and one large transport are parked at the end of a grass-covered runway.

Next to the transport, you notice a woman and a young boy being taken out of a car by two men in khaki fatigues. They look hypnotized. With a start, you recognize Mrs. Wilson and Buzzy Hargrove! You haven't been spotted, and you've got to do something fast.

Turn to page 101.

"I wouldn't join your organization," you say. "You're nothing but a bunch of terrorists."

"I can see now that there is nothing we can do to help you. Nurse, get Carlos," Dr. Cranshaw says, stomping out of the infirmary.

The nurse leaves, and for a few moments you are alone. Desperately you struggle with the straps holding you down. You manage to get one of them loose just as Carlos comes in.

"So, you are the stubborn one," he says. "I admire that. I too am the same way. Perhaps one day I will let you go. But not just yet. I'll need you until my new order has risen to take over the world." Then he laughs diabolically. Carlos goes out of the infirmary as two of his guards come in to make sure you don't try anything.

How long will it be before you can escape from this madman? you wonder. Looking around at the guards and the stone walls of the caverns, you know it's not going to be anytime soon.

The End

ABOUT THE AUTHOR

RICHARD BRIGHTFIELD is a graduate of Johns Hopkins University, where he studied biology, psychology, and archaeology. For many years he worked as a graphic designer at Columbia University. He has written many books in the Choose Your Own Adventure series, including *Planet of the Dragons, Hurricane!, Master of Kung Fu,* and *Master of Tae Kwon Do.* In addition, Mr. Brightfield has coauthored more than a dozen game books with his wife, Glory. The Brightfields and their daughter, Savitri, live in Gardiner, New York.

ABOUT THE ILLUSTRATOR

FRANK BOLLE studied at Pratt Institute. He has worked as an illustrator for many national magazines and now creates and draws cartoons for magazines as well. He has also worked in advertising and children's educational materials and has drawn and collaborated on several newspaper comic strips, including *Annie* and *Winnie Winkle.* Most recently he has illustrated *The Case of the Silk King, Longhorn Territory, Track of the Bear, Exiled to Earth, Master of Kung Fu, South Pole Sabotage, Return of the Ninja, You Are a Genius, Through the Black Hole, The Worst Day of Your Life, Master of Tae Kwon Do,* and *The Cobra Connection* in the Choose Your Own Adventure series. A native of Brooklyn Heights, New York, Mr. Bolle now lives and works in Westport, Connecticut.

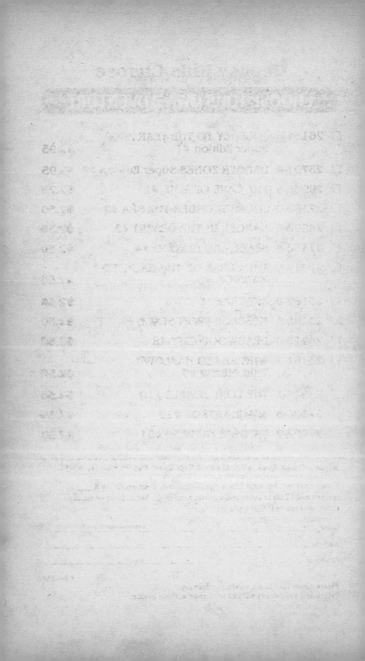

Choosy Kids Choose

CHOOSE YOUR OWN ADVENTURE ®

CHOOSE YOUR OWN ADVENTURE ®

☐ 26983-6 **GHOST HUNTER #52** $2.50

☐ 27565-8 **SECRET OF THE NINJA #66** $2.50

☐ 26723-X **SPACE VAMPIRE #71** $2.50

☐ 26725-6 **BEYOND THE GREAT WALL #73** $2.50

☐ 26904-6 **LONG HORN TERRITORY #74** $2.50

☐ 26887-2 **PLANET OF DRAGONS #75** $2.50

☐ 27004-4 **MONA LISA IS MISSING #76** $2.50

☐ 27063-X **FIRST OLYMPICS #77** $2.50

☐ 27123-7 **RETURN TO ATLANTIS #78** $2.50

☐ 26950-X **MYSTERY OF THE SACRED STONES #79** $2.50

Bantam Books, Dept. AV, 414 East Golf Road, Des Plaines, IL 60016

Please send me the items I have checked above. I am enclosing $_____
(please add $2.00 to cover postage and handling). Send check or money
order, no cash or C.O.D.s please.

Mr/Ms _____

Address _____

City/State _____ Zip _____

AV—9/90

Please allow four to six weeks for delivery.
Prices and availability subject to change without notice.